W9-BVT-542

E FIC   Numberman Neil   c.1
Numberman, Neil.
Do not build a Franken-
stein!

PROPERTY OF
HIGH POINT PUBLIC LIBRARY
HIGH POINT, NORTH CAROLINA

Do Not Build a Frankenstein!

Do Not Build a Frankenstein!

by Neil Numberman

Greenwillow Books

An Imprint of HarperCollinsPublishers

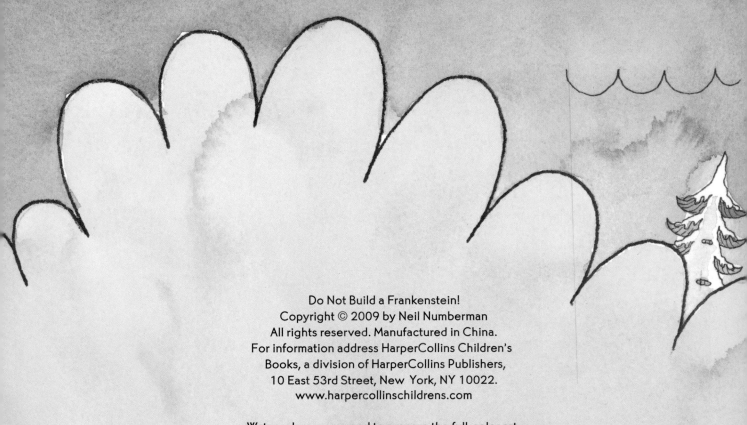

Do Not Build a Frankenstein!
Copyright © 2009 by Neil Numberman
All rights reserved. Manufactured in China.
For information address HarperCollins Children's
Books, a division of HarperCollins Publishers,
10 East 53rd Street, New York, NY 10022.
www.harpercollinschildrens.com

Watercolors were used to prepare the full-color art.
The text type is Martin Gothic.

Library of Congress Cataloging-in-Publication Data
Numberman, Neil.
Do not build a Frankenstein! / by Neil Numberman.
    p. cm.
"Greenwillow Books."
Summary: A boy warns his new neighbors of the trouble that comes
with building a monster, including having to move to a different town
in hopes of escaping his creation.
ISBN 978-0-06-156816-9 (trade bdg.) — ISBN 978-0-06-156817-6 (lib. bdg.)
[1. Monsters—Fiction. 2. Moving, Household—Fiction.] I. Title.
PZ7.N96356Do 2009   [E]—dc22   2008020751

First Edition 09 10 11 12 13 SCP 10 9 8 7 6 5 4 3 2 1

 Greenwillow Books

To Ryan and Connor,
the Frankenfamily

Gather round! Gather round!
I have very important advice to give!

Trust me. I know. I tried.
You must dedicate your entire life
to building a Frankenstein.

You must research . . .

build a laboratory . . .

and find the right parts.

At first, having a Frankenstein may be fun.

But after a while . . .

it can become pretty annoying.

He'll chase away your friends . . .

and your pets . . .

and he'll break all your toys.

He'll follow you everywhere . . .

and pretend that he's not.

Even when you try to ignore him,
he keeps bothering you.

All you can do is move away,
to a new town full of new people.

So friends, I'm begging you.
Take my advice . . .

GASP!